I Love You Like...

Lori Joy Smith

Owlkids Books

I love you...

Like forests love a seed,

Like plants love to grow,

Like flowers love the sun,

Like the grass loves a breeze.

I love you...

Like clouds love to fly,

Like a kiss loves a cheek,

Like the ocean loves the beach,

Like balloons love the sky.

I love you...

Like raindrops love a puddle,

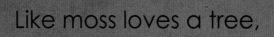

Like moss loves a tree,

Like mushrooms love the shade,

Like fur loves a cuddle.

I love you...

Like gnomes love to hide,

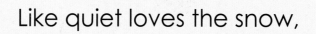

Like quiet loves the snow,

Like a pillow loves to sleep,

Like the moon loves the night.